Word List

Here is a list of words that might make it easier
to read this book. You'll find them in boldface
the first time they appear in the story.

assembly	uh-SEM-blee
costume	KOS-toom
permanent	PER-muh-nent
certainty	SER-tuhn-tee
mischievous	MIS-chuh-vuhs
caterpillar	KA-tuh-pi-ler
antennae	an-TE-nuh
transferred	TRANS-ferd
awkwardly	AW-kwerd-lee
contestant	kuhn-TES-tuhnt
Colossal	kuh-LO-suhl

Friendship, Not for Sale

Published by Grolier Books, a division of Grolier Enterprises, Inc.
Story by Linda Williams Aber. Photo crew: Willy Lew, Mary Hirahara, Dave Bateman, Steve Alfano, and Judy Tsuno.
Produced by Bumpy Slide Books.
Printed in the United States of America.
ISBN: 0-7172-8888-9

GROLIER
B O O K S

Chapter One

Stacie and Katie stood in the doorway of the lunchroom, waving excitedly to their friends. "Hurry up!" Stacie called to Janet and Whitney. "We have important stuff to talk about today!"

"We're coming!" Janet called back as she walked quickly toward Stacie and Katie.

Whitney hurried to catch up to Janet. "Come on," she said, giving Stacie a gentle push. "Let's get lunch before someone else grabs our table."

Stacie moved forward in the line. Katie, Whitney, and Janet were lined up behind her. They slid their trays along the tray track, chattering excitedly as they went. They were in the same third-grade class together, but this was their favorite time of the day. When the lunch bell rang, they always raced to the lunchroom. They always waited in line together. And they always sat together at the same table.

The four girls had been best friends for so long that they had formed a Best Friends' Club. And there was always something for the Best Friends' Club to talk about at its table.

Their table looked just like all the other tables in the big lunchroom. But because it was "their" table, it was special to them. It was in a corner next to a wall. Because it was off to the side, they didn't get bumped by all the other kids rushing by with full lunch trays.

The girls moved quickly along the lunch line. They each took a hamburger, a yogurt, a piece of fruit, cookies, and a bottle of water.

"Trade you my peach for your cookies,"

Stacie said to Whitney.

Whitney laughed. "Stacie!" she said. "You know I never change my mind about the cookies. You ask me every day, and I always say the same thing. 'Thanks, but no thanks!'"

"Oh, well," Stacie giggled. "One of these days, you just might change your mind."

"Never!" Whitney laughed. Suddenly she stopped in her tracks. "Oh, no!" she cried. "Look! Those boys took our table!"

The other girls turned their attention to their usual table. Sure enough, Whitney was right. Four boys from the fourth grade had their trays spread over the table. They were chomping on sandwiches and flipping potato chips across the table at one another.

"Look at that!" Janet moaned. "They're making a mess!"

"Oh, well," Stacie shrugged, trying to make the best of things. "Maybe they won't sit there tomorrow. Anyway, there's a better table over by the window." She led the way and sat down at the new table.

"I like the other table better," Whitney complained, following Stacie. "It's always been ours!"

"This one isn't so bad," Stacie said as she opened her bottle of water. "If we eat here from now on, we can watch the fall leaves change colors," she continued. "Maybe we'll even make new friends."

"We don't need new friends," Whitney declared. She set down her tray. "We've got each other."

"Never mind the table," Janet told the group. "Let's get back to the Halloween contest!"

There was an air of excitement throughout the whole school. The principal, Mrs. Hanson, had made a special announcement at the all-school **assembly** that morning.

"I can't wait!" Katie squealed. "There's going to be a Halloween party and a **costume** contest. This will be the best Halloween ever at school!"

"It sure will be," Whitney agreed.

"We have to think of the most BOO-tiful costume ideas ever," Janet said in a spooky-sounding voice.

"I definitely don't want to be a princess, witch, or cowgirl this year," Stacie declared.

"You're right," Janet agreed. "Last year there were four witches on my street alone. And I was one of them!"

"But yours was the best witch costume," Katie defended Janet. "Remember your green face?"

"Remember it?" Janet laughed. "How could I forget it? I had to see it in the mirror every day for a whole week after Halloween was over!"

"But we all learned a lesson from your mistake," Stacie giggled. "Use real makeup, not **permanent** markers!"

The four friends laughed together.

"Well, we're going to win the costume contest this year!" Whitney announced with **certainty.**

"You mean *one* of us is going to win," Janet corrected her. "We can't all win."

"Hmmm," Whitney sighed. She tilted her head to one side, the way she always did when she was thinking extra hard. "If we all enter the contest in different costumes, we'll be in a contest against each other."

"That's not good," Stacie said. "Somebody will end up mad."

"Or sad," Katie added.

"Or both," Janet finished.

"I've got it!" Whitney exclaimed, jumping

up from her seat.

BRrrrrriiing!

Before Whitney could say any more, the bell rang. Lunchtime was over.

"Got what?" Stacie asked on the way out of the lunchroom.

Whitney smiled a **mischievous** smile. "I've got the *best* idea," she declared.

The other girls begged her to tell them what she was thinking. Whitney pressed her lips together tightly and shook her head no. Then she burst into giggles. "I'm saving my idea for later!" she called out over the noise of kids hurrying back to their classrooms.

"You always make everything a big mystery!" Stacie scolded Whitney.

But Whitney just smiled. "I'll tell you tonight at my sleepover!" she explained. "You're going to love this idea. I promise!"

Chapter Two

Whitney was waiting at the door when
Stacie, Katie, and Janet arrived together. Her
smile, mischievous at lunch, had turned to a
smile of pure excitement. "I thought you'd never
get here!" she exclaimed, hurrying them inside.
"I can't wait another second to tell you my idea!"

Now it was Stacie's turn to tease Whitney
by keeping the suspense going. "Not yet,
Whitney," she joked, moving as slowly as
possible. "We need to set up our sleeping bags
first." She tossed her sleeping bag down the
stairs to the basement playroom.

"And then maybe we can have a snack or something," Janet added, keeping the joke going. She threw her sleeping bag down the stairs, too.

"Or why don't we just go right to sleep and you can tell us in the morning?" Katie suggested. She tossed her stuff down on top of the other girls' things.

Then Stacie, Katie, and Janet walked as slowly as they could down the stairs to the basement.

"Hey!" Whitney cried, following her guests. "Don't you want to hear my idea?"

At the bottom of the stairs, the girls couldn't carry on their teasing for another moment.

"Tell us!" Stacie squealed excitedly. "Of course we want to hear!"

The three girls flopped down on their bundled sleeping bags and waited for Whitney to tell them her idea. Whitney stood in front of them and took a deep breath. "Well," she said at last, "if we each have our own costume, only one of us can win. But if we're all wearing the same costume, we'll all win!"

"What?" Stacie cried, disappointed. "You mean we'll all be princesses, or rock stars, or witches, or whatever?"

"That's not such a great idea," Janet complained.

"Well, it's not a terrible idea," Katie offered, trying not to hurt Whitney's feelings.

Whitney laughed. "No, you sillies." She explained, "I mean we'll all go as the same *one* thing. We could all be together inside one costume. And it has to be something just right for four. That's why we're going to be one giant **caterpillar**!"

"Yes!" Stacie cheered. "That's a great idea!"

"Nobody else would think of that in a million years!" Janet exclaimed happily.

"In a billion years!" Stacie added.

"We'll be the only best-friends caterpillar in the contest!" Katie declared.

"And we can be any kind of caterpillar we like," Whitney continued, "because we'll make the costume ourselves!"

Everyone agreed. Then the girls changed into their pajamas and set up their sleeping bags in a circle. Whitney brought down a tray carrying a big bowl of popcorn, drinks, and a supply of colored markers and paper. The girls lay on their stomachs and propped themselves up on their elbows. From that moment on, they were costume designers.

They drew fat caterpillars, skinny caterpillars, striped ones, polka-dotted ones, and caterpillars of every color. When they had enough drawings to cover one wall of the playroom, they stopped.

"Now it's time to choose the best design," Whitney said, tacking the last drawing to the

corkboard wall.

"They're all the best!" Katie exclaimed.

"Then we'll just have to choose the best of the best," Stacie laughed. Then she wriggled across the room caterpillar-style inside her sleeping bag. When she had inched her way over to the wall,

 Stacie stood up. "I pick this one!" she announced, pointing to the wildest design on the wall. It was a plump, green caterpillar with yellow spots on one middle section, red spots on the other middle section, two **antennae** on the head, and a yellow, fuzzy pom-pom on the back end.

"Me, too," Janet said.

"That's my favorite one, too," Katie agreed. "Who did it?"

Whitney smiled a champion's smile. "I did!" she beamed.

"Whitney," Stacie began, "I think you should be the head of the caterpillar, since you had the idea in the first place."

"Okay, but it will take all four of us to make the caterpillar move," Whitney replied.

"How will we make it?" Katie asked.

"Stacie, can you get your sister Barbie to help?" Whitney asked hopefully. "She's made lots of costumes, hasn't she?"

Stacie swelled with pride. Barbie was good at a lot of things, but costume-making was one of her best talents. "I'll ask her when she picks me up in the morning," Stacie answered with a big yawn.

Stacie's yawn started the other girls yawning, too. It had been an exciting day, but a long one. The girls snuggled deep into their sleeping bags. They talked until the last one of them had finally fallen asleep.

In the morning, Barbie's voice woke them.

"Wake up, sleepyheads!" Barbie called as she walked down the stairs. "Wow!" she exclaimed when she saw the wall filled with designs for the caterpillar costume. "You girls have been busy! No wonder you're still sleeping!"

All four girls jumped up and started talking at once. Barbie listened and tried to understand what they were all saying. "Wait a minute!" she laughed when they finally took a breath. "So you're making a caterpillar costume, and you want me to help?"

"Exactly!" Stacie said excitedly. She hugged her big sister. "Say yes, please!"

"I'd love to help!" Barbie exclaimed. "I have a trunk full of fabrics and supplies in our basement." She was already thinking of ways to make the costume match the design. "Why don't you all come over now, and we'll get started right away?"

The girls called their parents and got dressed

in minutes. After a quick breakfast, they thanked Whitney's mother and went to Barbie and Stacie's house.

"Look at this great stuff!" Katie squealed. She pulled out a bag of feathers and sequins from the trunk. "We'll be the best-dressed caterpillar in the world!"

"Of course you will be," Barbie stated. She held up a piece of green velvet that was just the right length to make the body. "How's this?" she asked.

"Never mind that," Janet said, looking through a second trunk. "What's *this?*"

Janet was holding up a hot pink minidress with a sparkly silver belt. "Did you really wear this?" Janet asked Barbie.

"More than once," Barbie replied with a laugh. "More like once a week! That was one of my favorite outfits."

"Well," Whitney said, giggling, "all I can

say is, I'm glad fashions have changed!"

"So am I!" Barbie agreed. "Some changes are definitely for the best."

Once everything had been pulled out of the trunks, the girls were ready to start working on the costume. The green velvet was perfect for the body of the caterpillar.

"First you have to measure it. Then you can cut it," Barbie explained, giving them pointers on costume-making.

While Stacie and Whitney worked on the green fabric, Katie and Janet were busy cutting big yellow and red spots from felt. Once everything had been cut, Barbie showed them how to pin it together. After a full morning of work, the costume was pinned together and ready for them to try on.

"Ta da!" Stacie yelled as they all finally stood holding up the pinned-together costume. "How do we look?"

Barbie couldn't hide her giggles. The caterpillar costume was a long way from finished. But with a little work, it was going to be terrific!

Chapter Three

Designing the caterpillar costume on paper turned out to be the easiest part. Finding a time when all four girls could meet after school to sew it together was a lot harder.

Stacie had soccer practice. Janet had to walk her dog. Whitney spent her free time taking piano lessons and practicing. And Katie had ballet class.

"We'll never get the costume done if we don't work on it together," Stacie declared. "Next Saturday has to be costume day, no matter what!"

Everyone agreed to meet at Stacie's house

at ten o'clock on Saturday morning. Katie and Janet showed up right on time. Stacie led them to the room where the green velvet costume was spread out on the floor.

"Gosh," Katie sighed, looking at the limp material. "It sure doesn't look like a winning costume yet!"

"You're right about that," Stacie agreed. "We still have lots to do. I wish Whitney would get here. I wonder what's taking her so long?"

"We might as well get started," Janet said. "At least we can work on the body. When Whitney comes, we can put the head together."

"You make us sound like mad scientists or something," Katie giggled. "We're creating a caterpillar, not a monster, you know!"

Stacie tossed a scrap of green velvet over her head. "Aarrrgh!" she growled, pretending to take a swipe at Katie with a clawed hand.

"Yikes!" Katie cried. "It's a Stacie-monster!"

"Very funny," Stacie laughed, pulling off the fabric.

Stacie, Katie, and Janet were rolling on the floor laughing when Whitney walked in.

"Hi, Whitney!" Stacie greeted her between giggles. "What took you so long?"

"What's wrong?" Katie asked seriously. "You look like you've seen a ghost!"

"Or maybe just a giant green caterpillar!" Janet joked.

Whitney didn't laugh. Tears welled up in her eyes as she stood in the doorway with her coat still on. "I . . . I . . . ," she started to say.

"What is it?" Janet and Stacie asked together.

"I'm moving away!" Whitney finally blurted out. Now the tears poured down her cheeks, and her story poured out with them. "My dad is being **transferred** for his job!" she sobbed. "Our whole family has to move to another state!"

"No!" Katie gasped, her mouth dropping

open. "But why? What's wrong with the job he has here?"

"My mom says the new job is too good to pass up, and we have to go," Whitney tried to explain.

The caterpillar costume was forgotten as all the girls started talking at once.

"This can't really happen," Janet protested. "Your parents will change their minds when they see how sad you are."

"They can't do this to you!" Katie cried. "They can't do this to *us!*"

"Wait a minute! Wait a minute!" Stacie began. As usual, Stacie tried to make the best out of a bad situation. "Maybe you have to think of the move as an adventure, Whitney! You'll be seeing a new place and meeting new people."

But this didn't make Whitney feel better.

And then Janet said the worst thing of all. "Hey! If you move, our caterpillar costume will

25

be ruined. We'll never win the contest!"

Janet's words really hurt Whitney. "You mean all you care about is winning the stupid contest? I'm not even moving until after Halloween!" Whitney shouted, stamping her foot. "It's not my fault I'm moving. But maybe it's a good thing, after all! You three can be in the caterpillar costume by yourselves. I don't want to be in it anymore!"

Before the girls could stop her, Whitney turned and ran out. As the bad news sank in, each of them grew sadder.

But Whitney was the saddest of all. Walking home, she thought about the awful truth. Everything was changing—the table at school, the leaves, Halloween plans. And now her whole life was about to change!

Whitney slammed the door behind her when she got home. She sat down on the stairs and buried her head in her lap. "Why is this happening to me?" she groaned.

A comforting hand touched her shoulder. "Oh, Whitney," her mom said in a soft voice. "It's not only happening to you. It's happening to all of us. I know how sad you feel, because I feel sad, too. We'll all have to adjust. But I promise I'll do my best to make it easier for you."

"What could make losing my best friends easier?" Whitney cried into her mother's shoulder.

Her mother tried to sound cheerful. "We'll get you your own e-mail address so you can keep in touch!"

But Whitney remembered how Stacie had said they'd make new friends when they'd had to change tables in the lunchroom. "E-mail won't help," she said tearfully. "They'll forget me as soon as we move. They have each other, and I won't have anyone at all!"

"Whitney," her mother replied patiently, "change is never easy. But no matter where we go, our family will always be together. Our house may change, but our home will always be where our family is. I hope you'll try to find the silver lining in the cloud."

Whitney wiped a tear from her cheek and looked at her mother. She was surprised to see her mother wiping a tear away, too.

"I'll try to look for the silver lining in the cloud," Whitney promised her mother. But she thought to herself that the cloud looked just like a big, dark rain cloud.

Chapter Four

The For Sale sign on her front lawn made the cloud hanging over Whitney seem even heavier and darker. As family after family marched through her house to see if they'd like to buy it, Whitney felt sadder and sadder.

"I can't stand keeping my room neat all the time!" Whitney told the girls at lunch one day.

"You can stay over at my house until your house is sold," Stacie offered.

Whitney exploded in anger. "What?" she exclaimed. "And leave my house for some other family to come and take over? You just don't understand!"

Before the rest of the girls could say anything, Whitney got up from the table and ran out of the lunchroom.

"Gee," Stacie said sadly to the others, "I didn't mean to upset her."

Stacie wanted to talk to Whitney after lunch and say she was sorry. But Whitney had gone to the nurse's office and then home.

After school, Stacie called Whitney. "I'm sorry, Stacie," Whitney's mother apologized. "Whitney isn't feeling well. She's asleep now. I'll have her call you when she wakes up."

But Whitney didn't call back. And for the next two days, Whitney wasn't at school. When she finally did come back, she wasn't her usual self at all. Whitney didn't talk to her friends in class. Instead of waiting in the lunch line with them, she brought her lunch from home. Instead of eating with them, she ate alone in the music room. And after school, Whitney rushed home without saying good-bye to any of them.

"I don't get it," Janet sighed, shaking her head. "Why doesn't Whitney want to be with us?"

"I don't know," Katie said sadly. "It's even more important now to spend time together. We don't have much time left!"

"We have to talk to her!" Stacie exclaimed.

That day after school, Stacie, Katie, and Janet went straight to Whitney's house. When they got there, the three girls gasped in surprise. The For Sale sign was still there. But beneath it, in big, black letters, was the word *SOLD*.

"Oh, no!" Katie cried.

Stacie ran to the door and rang the bell. "Is Whitney home?" she asked when Whitney's mother answered.

"No," her mother replied. "Whitney's dad picked her up at school. They're out doing some errands. I'm on the telephone right now, but

please come in and wait. She'll be back soon."

The girls stepped inside and waited in the living room while Whitney's mother returned to the telephone.

"Look!" Janet exclaimed. She pointed to stacks of boxes lined up against the wall. Two whole stacks were labeled *Whitney's Room.*

"It's all of Whitney's stuff!" Stacie cried.

"This is terrible," Katie said softly. "How can a person's life be packed into boxes so easily?"

"I don't think it was so easy, Katie," Stacie replied. "No wonder we haven't seen Whitney much. She's probably been too busy packing all these boxes."

"I can't believe it," Janet sighed. "Whitney really is moving away."

Just then the front door opened, and Whitney came in. "What are you doing here?" she cried.

"Hi," Stacie said **awkwardly.** "We were just stopping by to see if we could help you pack."

Whitney brushed past them and headed up the stairs to her room. The other girls followed her.

Whitney pointed to more boxes packed and ready to go. "You can see I don't need any help packing. It's all done!"

"Whitney," Stacie began, "why have you been avoiding us? We save a place for you in the lunch line and at our table. We wait for you after school. We . . ."

"We miss you!" Janet blurted out. "You're supposed to be the head of our whole caterpillar costume! We're your friends, and you're acting like you've already moved! It's not fair for you to treat us this way!"

"Fair?" Whitney shouted angrily at Janet. "Nothing's fair! Everything is changing. Nothing's fair at all anymore!"

Janet had no reply for Whitney. Feeling hurt and angry herself, Janet stamped out of the room and ran down the stairs.

Katie and Stacie were hurt, too. They followed Janet. "You're right, Whitney," Stacie said sadly on her way out. "Nothing's fair at all anymore."

Chapter Five

Without Whitney in the costume, Katie and Janet didn't want to work on it anymore. It was Stacie who insisted that they meet at her house and try to get more done.

"Halloween is only a few days away," Stacie reminded them. "If we don't have this costume, we won't have *any* costume!"

"Halloween was going to be so great this year," Katie complained. "We were going to have the best costume in the contest."

Stacie held up the large yellow spot she was sewing onto the green velvet. "We'll still have the best costume," she told them. "We just won't have enough people inside of it."

"Whitney never should have quit on us," Janet grumbled, poking her needle into a fluffy pom-pom. "We'll never finish on time. We need her!"

"Call her, Janet," Stacie suggested. "Tell her we're saving the head for her. Tell her if she doesn't help sew the head, we'll be the only headless caterpillar in the world."

"I'll try," Janet agreed. She went to the phone in the kitchen and was back in less than two minutes. "She can't come over," Janet said. "Her mom needs her to help clean out the basement."

All three girls sighed.

"Why all the sad faces?" Barbie asked, peeking in to see how the costume-making was going. She was surprised to see the caterpillar costume only half-done. "What happened?" she asked. "It's almost Halloween, and you're not even close to being finished!"

"It's all Whitney's fault," Janet wailed. "She dropped out on us!"

"Dropped out?" Barbie exclaimed. "But why? It was her idea!"

"Ever since Whitney found out that she's moving, she's changed," Stacie explained. "She didn't only drop the costume. She dropped us, too!"

Barbie sat down on the floor with the girls and picked up a needle and thread. "Why don't I help you a little bit?" she offered.

As they sewed the costume, Barbie tried to explain how Whitney might feel. "Moving away must be very hard for Whitney and her family. They have to change houses, change schools, change jobs, and . . ."

". . . Change friends," Janet finished.

"Whitney won't change friends," Barbie

said. "But let's hope she *adds* new friends. You girls and Whitney have been best friends all your lives. Where she lives won't change that fact. But it's up to you to make sure Whitney knows that you won't forget her. You have to remind her that there will always be a place saved for her in your group. Just like there's a space for her in this caterpillar costume."

"But she doesn't want to be in the group or in the costume anymore!" Katie cried.

"It may seem that way," Barbie replied. "But everyone has a different way of reacting to a change as big as moving."

"Well, I know how I'm reacting," Katie pointed out. "I'm sad!"

"I want everything to be back the way it was," Stacie added.

"And what about you, Janet?" Barbie asked. "How do you feel about all this?"

Janet thought for a few seconds. "I guess I

just didn't want to believe it," she finally answered. "But when I saw the boxes all packed, I knew it really was true."

"And how do you think Whitney is feeling?" Barbie asked all the girls.

"She acts angry about it," Janet replied.

"And sad," Katie said.

"Maybe she just wishes everything would be back the way it was," Stacie finished.

"I think all of you are right," Barbie told the girls. "And all of those feelings are important."

"I guess we've all been so busy thinking about how we feel that we haven't thought about how Whitney feels," Janet realized.

"But what can we do?" Stacie asked. "We can't stop her family from moving away."

"No," Barbie told her sister. "But we can try to make Whitney feel better. I have a plan that I think will help Whitney *and* all of you. The first thing we're going to do is finish this costume. And then we'll start working on a surprise for Whitney!"

For the first time since they'd heard the news about Whitney moving, her three friends didn't feel helpless. Making a surprise that would make Whitney feel better made them feel better, too.

Chapter Six

For the next two days, Stacie, Katie, and Janet were too busy to feel bad. With Barbie's encouragement, they worked hard to finish the caterpillar costume. They wanted to do all the sewing by themselves, so Barbie left them alone to work.

Stacie finally made the last stitch in the caterpillar costume. She cut the thread and held up the head of the costume.

"Barbie!" Stacie called out. "We've finished the costume!"

"Congratulations!" Barbie said happily

when she entered the room.

Barbie examined the costume from antennae to pom-pom. The body was lumpy and slightly lopsided. The face was crooked, too. But the costume was a masterpiece to the girls who had made it.

"Wait until Whitney sees this!" Janet exclaimed. "It looks just like her drawing!"

"When Whitney sees the costume, she'll want to be in it, too," Stacie added.

"I hope so," Katie said. "We're sure to win!"

"Just to be safe," Barbie suggested, "why don't you try it on and see how it looks?"

The three girls carefully slipped the costume on over their heads. Stacie took Whitney's place and stuck her head inside the big, green headpiece. Janet's job was to hold up the fluffy pom-pom end. Katie held up the whole middle part by sticking one arm out in front and one arm out in back.

"I hope the contest judges don't take too

long to decide," Katie said. "My arms won't be able to stay out like this forever!"

"And it's hot inside this head!" Stacie's muffled voice cried. She slipped the head off and gasped for breath. "Whew! I never knew it would be so hard to be a caterpillar!"

Barbie couldn't hold her laughter in. "You girls did a great job," she said. "It's a wonderful caterpillar. But we don't have much time left. The contest and party are tomorrow, and we still have Whitney's surprise to work on."

This time the girls let Barbie help more. When the surprise was finally finished, they put it in a big gift box and tied it closed with a red ribbon. It was agreed that Barbie would bring the costume and Whitney's surprise gift to school in time for the contest after lunch.

The next day, Stacie, Katie, and Janet met at the door to the lunchroom as usual. "Wow!" Stacie exclaimed. "It doesn't even look like the lunchroom today!"

Paper bats, jack-o'-lanterns, and ghosts hung from the ceiling, peeked through the windows, and popped out from behind the stacks of lunch trays. Spooky music played over the loudspeaker. And instead of the usual line for lunch, one long table was set up with hot dogs, chips, cookies, fruit, and drinks.

The girls filled their trays with lunch. They went to their new table, which they'd all decided was much better than the old table. As they sat down, Janet spotted Whitney carrying a lunch tray.

Stacie saw her, too. "Whitney!" she shouted across the room. "Over here!"

Whitney slowly came toward the table. She was tired of being mad and tired of being sad.

She wanted to be with her friends. "Is there room for me?" she asked quietly.

"We've been saving you a seat for two weeks!" Katie exclaimed. "Of course there's room!"

Janet and Whitney looked at each other and smiled awkwardly. Whitney sat down next to Janet. "Are you going to bob for apples?" Janet asked her, trying to act normal.

"I guess so," Whitney replied. "Are you?"

"Sure she is!" Stacie bubbled happily. She was so glad to have all four seats at the table filled again. "We're going to do everything," Stacie declared. "Apple bobbing, pumpkin decorating, Pat the Bat, everything! It's Halloween!"

But it was the costume contest that they were really waiting for. "Just wait until you see our caterpillar costume," Janet told Whitney. "It turned out great!"

"Look!" Stacie exclaimed, pointing toward the door. "There's Barbie with the costume now!"

Barbie waved from the doorway. All four girls ran over to greet her. "Hurry now," Barbie said, leading them to a classroom that was set up to be the girls' changing room. "You'll need a little extra time to get into this costume."

When the caterpillar costume was out of the bag, Whitney couldn't believe her eyes. "It's perfect!" she cried.

"We still want you to be the head of it," Janet insisted.

"Please?" Stacie begged.

Whitney smiled and nodded eagerly. "Okay!" she replied.

"Great!" Katie cheered. "Now my arms won't fall off!"

With Barbie's help, all four girls slipped into the costume. Even with four of them inside, the green caterpillar looked a little lopsided. But the girls didn't care. They practiced walking in the costume and burst into giggles. No matter how hard they tried, they couldn't get their legs all going in the same direction at the same time. And Katie and Stacie got squashed when Janet kept walking after Whitney had stopped. Before they were really ready, they heard the announcement for the contest to begin.

The four girls marched out the door and into the lunchroom. They quickly lined up and pulled the costume over their heads.

"Here goes nothing!" Whitney called out from inside the head.

On the count of three from Barbie, the four caterpillar parts began to march. Following the judges' orders, the caterpillar bumped and bumbled its way around the costume parade area.

"Thank you all!" Mrs. Hanson, the principal, said after the last **contestant** had passed by the judges. "And the prize for the best costume this year goes to . . . Greg Garrison for his **Colossal** Computer Chip costume!"

"What?" all four girls cried out in muffled voices.

"You mean we didn't win?" Katie asked, ducking out of the costume.

"I can't believe it!" Stacie shouted.

But Janet and Whitney couldn't stop laughing. They were tangled up in the costume and couldn't get out!

The caterpillar's beginning and end wrestled wildly until Whitney and Janet were free at last. As Stacie and Katie watched this, they forgot about losing. While Greg Garrison walked up to claim his prize, the four giggling girls hugged one another like the best friends they had always been and always would be.

"Hey, I almost forgot!" Stacie cried, breaking away from the group hug. "We have a surprise for you, Whitney!"

Barbie handed Stacie, Katie, and Janet the box. Janet presented it to Whitney. "Open it!" she said excitedly.

Whitney opened the box. She took out a glittering pair of butterfly wings made of pink and blue fabric. Sparkling jewels were sewn all around the edges.

"They're beautiful!" Whitney exclaimed, slipping the wings onto her arms. "I'm a butterfly!"  she cried, waving her arms up and down gracefully.

"That's what caterpillars change into, Whitney," Barbie explained. "Not all changes are bad. Sometimes change is beautiful!"

"I'm going to miss you all so much," Whitney said with tears in her eyes. "But I won't forget where I came from, no matter what else changes. I'll come back to visit a lot."

"And the Best Friends' Club will hold a special meeting every time you do," Katie added.

"We'll always be best friends, no matter where any of us live," Whitney declared.

"Promise?" asked Janet.

"Promise," replied Whitney.

"Trade you my peach for your cookies?" Stacie joked before things got too serious.

"Thanks, but no thanks!" Whitney laughed. "Some things will never change. Ever!"